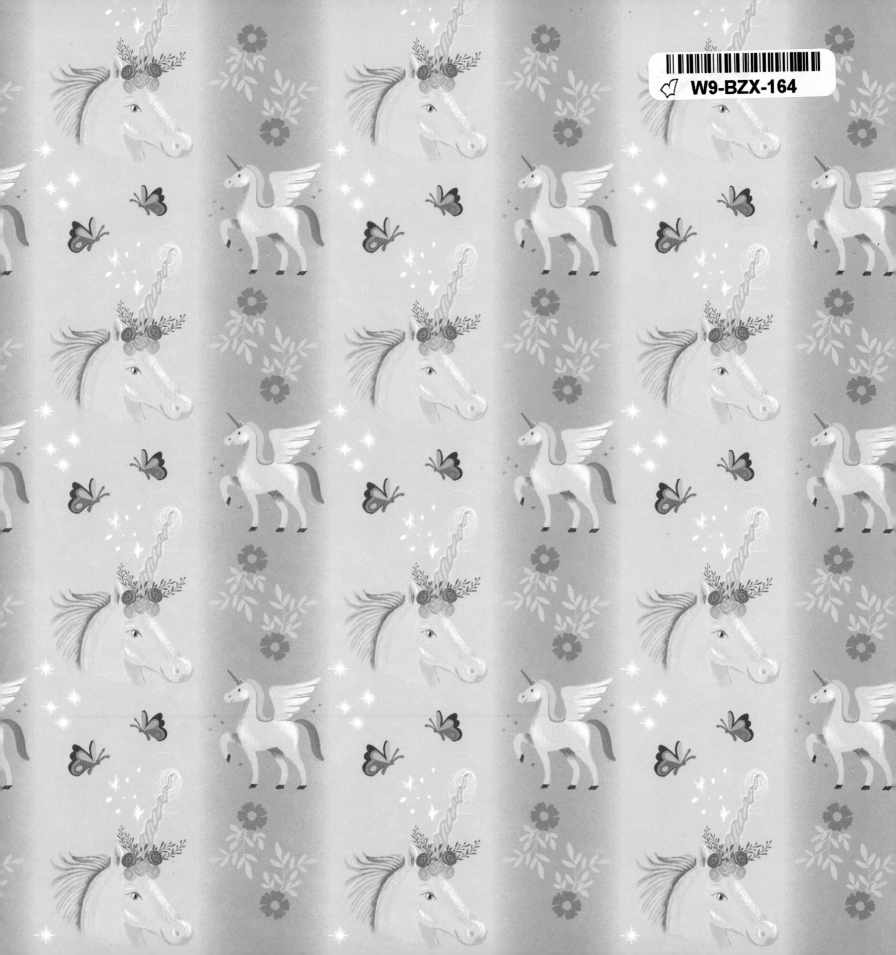

# THE MAGIC OF UNICORNS

By Gina L. Grandi · Illustrated by Ximena Jeria

downtown bookworks

FOR DEVON AND AMALTHEA

downtown bookworks

Downtown Bookworks Inc.
265 Canal Street
New York, NY 10013
www.downtownbookworks.com

Designed by Georgia Rucker
Typeset in Caniste and Neutraface Slab

Printed in the United States
October 2018
ISBN 978-1-941367-61-2

10 9 8 7 6 5 4 3 2 1

𝒜 **FIELD GUIDE** is a book that teaches you about birds, insects, mammals, plants, or other things in nature: where to find them, how to identify them, and how they live. A *fabulous* field guide tells you everything you need to know about magical, mythical beings. This book is here to support you in your quest to learn all about unicorns: their habits, their powers, and the best way to go about finding one.

Are you an explorer? A scientist? A zoologist? An intelligent person who has a curious mind and is eager to know about the exciting world of fantastic creatures? You've come to the right place. If you're preparing for a unicorn expedition, pack your notebook and sketch pad, a water bottle, and a nutritious snack, and make sure you have on sturdy shoes. If you're reading cozily at home, slip on some fluffy socks and wrap up in a comfy blanket. Be sure to share this book with a friend—if you put your heads together, you just might succeed in spotting a unicorn.

Best of luck,

𝒢INA

# An Unforgettable Meeting

A young girl sits alone in a forest. She is very still, waiting.
After a moment, there's a rustle of leaves. The girl holds her
breath. The leaves part, and there is a flash of white. Is it a bird?
She looks closer. And she sees a flowing mane, a sparkling eye,
and then a gleaming, spiral horn. The unicorn moves into the
clearing. Carefully, cautiously, it steps toward the girl until
it's close enough to lower its lovely head and nuzzle her hair.
This unicorn has found someone it trusts, someone it
knows to be a friend.

The unicorn is one of the most well-known and
well-loved magical creatures in the world.

# The First Unicorns

When picturing a unicorn, most people think of a graceful, white animal with a golden horn coming out of its forehead. But you might be surprised to find out what the earliest unicorns looked like. The first unicorn-like creature ever written about was described more than two thousand years ago in a book written by a Greek doctor named Ctesias. The animals he wrote about lived in India. They were as large as horses and had white bodies, red heads, and mesmerizing blue eyes.

It's hard to imagine a unicorn with the thick legs of an elephant. But that's how Aelian, a writer and teacher in ancient Rome, described the same Indian "unicorns." He said they lived high in the mountains and had splendid multicolored horns. Aelian was also the first to describe the magical properties of a unicorn's horn.

# Lore of the Unicorn

Over the many years since the first unicorn sightings, curious people have traveled to new places. These explorers wrote books about who and what they encountered on their journeys. Poets sang about the fantastic creatures seen in far-off lands. Children heard these poems and songs and shared them with their friends. Tales of unicorns were passed from person to person, land to land, through songs and stories and books. These accounts reveal lots of information that will help you on your quest to spot a unicorn.

# Peaceful Creatures

Unicorns are powerful and swift, but even though their strength is mighty, they are gentle, loving beings. Their presence brings peace to the forests they roam, and they devote themselves to protecting the living things around them.

They spend most of their time alone, surrounded by the other animals of the woods, mountains, and meadows. Sometimes, they will approach a young girl and fall asleep in her lap. Even so, very few people have been lucky enough to see them. If you ever catch a glimpse of a unicorn, it won't be by accident. It will be because the unicorn has recognized you as someone special.

# Wild and Free

Unicorns are special creatures. And like all truly special things, they are rare. One of the reasons that seeing a unicorn is so difficult is because they usually live in remote, hard-to-reach places. The first unicorns were seen in the mountains. Others have been discovered deep in the forest or galloping like the wind through a sun-drenched meadow.

It isn't possible to tame a unicorn. A unicorn would never want to live in an apartment, or sleep in a bed, or wait by the door for you to come home from school. But even though you could never have a unicorn for a pet, you might one day have a unicorn for a friend.

# A Blessing of Unicorns

Unicorns are solitary animals. They love their fellow creatures, but they prefer to live alone. It would be an astounding event to come across a group of unicorns together. Writers have challenged themselves to come up with the right word to describe such a wondrous sight.

A group of seagulls is a flock, and a group of cows is a herd. Many call a group of unicorns a "blessing." Other writers choose to say a "glory" of unicorns or a "marvel" of unicorns. If you ever find yourself addressing a group of unicorns, perhaps the perfect word will come to you.

# Water and Wishes

A unicorn is so good, truthful, and pure that the touch of
its horn can cure any poison. In medieval Europe, kings, queens,
knights, and wealthy nobles would buy cups supposedly made
from unicorn horns to protect themselves against poison.

In the wild, unicorns use their magic to help their fellow animals.
When a unicorn dips its horn into a stream or lake, the water becomes
instantly purified so other animals can safely drink. Some stories say
that a unicorn's horn can even produce water. If a unicorn pierces a
rock with its horn, clean, refreshing water will come pouring out.

Unicorns are so strong and enchanting that just being near one
can bring a sense of joy and calm. There are even tales of
unicorns having the power to grant wishes.

# Tricksters, Beware!

Because unicorn horns are so extraordinary, fortune hunters throughout history have tried to catch unicorns in order to use or sell their horns. Maybe one of the reasons people don't see many unicorns today is because unicorns have learned to be wary of humans and don't come out of hiding often.

There are stories from long ago of hunters asking young girls to help them find unicorns. Most children were too kind to help cruel unicorn hunters. Still, some greedy men would search the woods in hopes of sneaking up and capturing a unicorn that had laid its head on a trustworthy girl's lap. Unicorns these days are far too clever to fall for tricks like this.

# QILIN WALK ON CLOUDS

The unicorn family tree has glorious beasts on all its branches. There are magical horned animals all over the world.

The one-horned **QILIN** has roamed China for thousands of years. It has the body of a deer and the hooves of a horse. Instead of fur or hair, the qilin is covered in shining scales, like a fish or a dragon. Although the qilin looks ferocious, it is actually very gentle. In fact, many stories say that the qilin walks only on clouds, in order to avoid hurting even a single blade of grass.

A qilin uses its magic to fill the hearts of honest people with happiness. It can breathe fire, but will only attack to protect someone in danger. Seeing a qilin is very good luck. If you find yourself in China, look up into the clouds. You might see the hooves of a qilin as it leaps above you.

# Kirin Are Fiery and Calm

Only the very fortunate have spotted the **KIRIN** in their adventures through the wilds of Japan. Like the qilin, the kirin is covered in scales. It may have a body like a lion instead of a deer. Usually gentle, the kirin can be fierce. It will seek out and find criminals, punishing them by piercing their hearts with its horn!

The kirin is called the King of the Land by those who believe it rules the universe with the phoenix (the King of Fire), the dragon (the King of the Air), and the tortoise (the King of the Water). Some people even say the first kirin appeared when two stars collided in the sky.

If you see a flash of orange light out of the corner of your eye while visiting Japan, it might just be the flames of a kirin's mane as it dashes by.

# Shy Abadas and Powerful Karkadanns

Can a unicorn have more than one horn? The mysterious African **ABADA** lives on the clay plains and in the hills of central Sudan and has two horns. Both horns have the same powers as the unicorn's single horn. The abada looks more like a donkey than a horse, but, like the unicorn, is very rare. You'll need extra patience if you want to meet an abada. They're even shyer than unicorns. Keep very still and quiet and think peaceful thoughts if you suspect an abada is nearby.

The **KARKADANN** can have up to three horns. You'll find it running wild across the grasslands of India and Persia, although you might think twice before stopping to say hello. The karkadann is a ferocious warrior with a huge body that shakes the ground when it walks. Keep your ears covered if you spot one coming: its loud bellow chases away all other animals. The only animal that doesn't fear the karkadann is the ring dove. This bird will even sit on a karkadann's horn and sing to it! If you're brave enough to face a karkadann, try singing it your favorite song—from a safe distance.

# Did an Emperor Meet a Unicorn?

Some famous historical figures have had their own unicorn encounters.

Genghis Khan was an emperor and warlord who lived 800 years ago. He traveled across central Asia and China, invading countries until he had conquered twice as much land as any person in history. Legend has it that in 1206, he was readying his forces to invade India. The troops were rallied. But as Genghis Khan prepared to attack, a unicorn appeared and bowed to him. He believed this was a sign to turn back, so he did, and India was saved.

# Wait, That's Not a Unicorn!

About 700 years ago, an Italian explorer named Marco Polo thought he had seen a black-horned unicorn while traveling through Sumatra. He was very disappointed in what he saw and reported that unicorns were not graceful and beautiful, but instead were huge, muddy, and clumsy. "They spend their time by preference wallowing in mud and slime," he wrote. It turns out he had seen a rhinoceros!

# Did a Unicorn Carry a King?

Alexander the Great was the king of Macedonia more than two thousand years ago. He led his army across Asia and Africa and created one of the largest empires of the ancient world. Alexander was a legendary military leader, and, astride his beloved warhorse Bucephalus, he was undefeated in battle. Some say that Bucephalus was not really a horse, but a unicorn. This mighty, thundering creature may have been a karkadann, which would explain why he was so fierce that no one but Alexander could ride him.

# COUSINS IN THE WATER

It's hard to picture a unicorn going for a swim, but these two unicorn-like creatures spend most of their time in the water.

The **NARWHAL** is a type of whale that lives in the Arctic. It doesn't look much like a unicorn, but it has a long tusk that resembles a unicorn's horn. Remember how, back in medieval times, kings, queens, and wealthy citizens bought cups and decorations made of unicorn horn? Those treasures usually turned out to be narwhal tusks!

A **KELPIE** is a magical Scottish water horse. Like the unicorn, kelpies prefer to live alone, but unlike unicorns, they are dangerous. Kelpies have the power to change their shape and sometimes transform themselves to look like humans in order to lure unsuspecting travelers into the water. Be cautious around lakes, rivers, and streams. If you see a swimming horse, keep your eyes open. If that horse suddenly morphs into a person, be on your guard. If that person invites you to join them in a game of water polo, decline politely. Then run away.

# Cousins in the Air

The unicorn has many cousins, both real and imaginary. Some of these unicorn-like creatures have one power the unicorn does not—they can fly!

A **HIPPOGRIFF** only resembles the unicorn from the waist down, where it has the body, hind legs, and tail of a horse. The head, wings, and front legs of a hippogriff are those of a giant eagle. Like the unicorn, the hippogriff is noble, strong, and a symbol of love and devotion. If you ever have the opportunity to meet a hippogriff, consider asking it respectfully to give you a ride. A flight with a hippogriff is just as wondrous as a gallop with a unicorn.

# The One and Only Pegasus!

Brave **Pegasus** is a winged horse from Greek mythology. One of Pegasus's most famous adventures was when he carried the hero Perseus to save the Princess Andromeda. Andromeda's mother made the mistake of saying that Andromeda was more beautiful than the sea nymphs, which angered the sea god Poseidon. It's never a good idea to make a Greek god angry. As punishment, Poseidon demanded that Andromeda be chained to a rock by the sea to be devoured by a sea monster. The faithful Pegasus flew Perseus to the rock, just in time for Perseus to cut Andromeda free. Then Pegasus swept them both safely away, his mighty wings carrying them high above the clutches of the fearsome monster.

Pegasus was also given the job of carrying thunderbolts for Zeus, king of the gods! And he was known for bringing inspiration to writers and poets.

Although there are many winged horses, there is only one Pegasus.

# WHERE ARE THEY NOW?

What have unicorns been up to since the days of Marco Polo and Alexander the Great? As the years passed, unicorns have become even more shy and reclusive. This might be because they were hunted for their horns and started to be careful to avoid humans. Our towns and cities have also become larger, taller, and noisier. They don't always provide the green and quiet unicorns prefer. There are not many stories about unicorn sightings these days—but that doesn't mean it isn't possible.

# How to
# Spot a Unicorn

Since unicorns live in the wild, your chances of seeing a unicorn are much better out in nature. Spend time learning about flowers, birds, and other animals. Even if you live in a city, get to know the trees in your neighborhood and visit the park as often as you can. Perhaps you'll find a one-horned statue while you're out for a stroll. Go on a hike with your family. Learn to be a friend of nature, and any unicorns that happen to be hiding nearby will start to see you as a friend of theirs as well.

Most stories say unicorns prefer to show themselves to girls— but maybe the right boy just hasn't come along yet.

# WHO CAN FIND A UNICORN?

Unicorns and other magical horned animals can tell the difference between good and evil. They like people who are kind and generous. Pay attention to the way you treat people. Are your actions thoughtful and considerate? Do you offer friendship to everyone? Do you stand up for what's right? A unicorn will know what's in your heart, and if you work at being loving and compassionate, it will be more likely to appear.

# SHOW SOME LOVE

If you don't live near a forest
or want to build up some good
deeds before starting your
search, you could always
let any unicorns around
know you appreciate
their majesty by
creating some art.
It never hurts to
appeal to a unicorn's
vanity. Consider
making a sketch of
a unicorn frolicking
in the woods,
a painting of a
unicorn napping
beneath a rainbow,
or a sculpture of a
unicorn meeting you
for the first time.

If you need inspiration for your own unicorn masterpiece, you can find images of unicorns in all kinds of places. You might find a unicorn in a museum or on a coat of arms. You might spot one at school. And there are always cuddly unicorns to take home.

# CELEBRATE
# NATIONAL UNICORN DAY
# EVERY DAY!

Just like you, unicorns love to be appreciated. The unicorn is the national animal of Scotland, and National Unicorn Day is celebrated there on April 9. But you don't need to wait until April. Unicorn Day can be the ninth of any month. Or the nineteenth. Or any day ending in "ay."

Unicorns are best celebrated with a rainbow cake (of course). Use your creative kitchen skills to bake something spectacular.

# Now and Forever

Unicorns have been with us for thousands of years. They roam the world, bringing love and protection. Even though they've been described in many ways in different times and places, they have always been rare and magnificent. Unicorns stand for goodness, freedom, and happiness.

Make friends with a tree, stand up for what's right, appreciate the beauty that's around you, and unicorn magic will bring you luck and happiness. Even if you haven't seen one ... yet.